W9-AOC-885

Rain Forests

Ted O'Hare

FITZGERALD
BOOKS

Bethany, Missouri

All rights reserved. This book, or parts thereof, may
not be reproduced, stored, or transmitted in
any form or by any means except by prior
written consent of the publisher.

Photo Credits:
Cover © Jonah Manning; Title Page © Photodisc; Page 5 © Catherine Scott; Pages 7, 17, 22 © Photodisc;
Page 9 © Patriek Vandenbussche; Page 10 © Michal Strzelecki; Page 11 © Mark Goble, Brazil2; Page 12 ©
Doxa; Page 13 © Gary Hotson; Page 14 © NOAA; Page 15 © Mike Bousquet, Eric Guinther; Page 16 ©
Micheal Sacco; Page 19 © Ye Liew; Page 21 © Brazil2

Cataloging-in-Publication Data

O'Hare, Ted, 1961-
    Rain forests / Ted O'Hare. — 1st ed.
    p. cm. — (Exploring habitats)

    Includes bibliographical references and index.
    Summary: Describes what rain forests are, where they are
found, and what types of plants and animals live there.
    ISBN-13: 978-1-4242-1385-6 (lib. bdg. : alk. paper)
    ISBN-10: 1-4242-1385-1 (lib. bdg. : alk. paper)
    ISBN-13: 978-1-4242-1475-4 (pbk. : alk. paper)
    ISBN-10: 1-4242-1475-0 (pbk. : alk. paper)

    1. Rain forests—Juvenile literature. 2. Rain forest ecology—
Juvenile literature. [1. Rain forests. 2. Rain forest plants.
3. Rain forest animals. 4. Rain forest ecology. 5. Ecology.]
I. O'Hare, Ted, 1961- II. Title.
III. Series.
    QH86.O43 2007
    577.34—dc22

First edition
© 2007 Fitzgerald Books
802 N. 41st Street, P.O. Box 505
Bethany, MO 64424, U.S.A.
Printed in China
Library of Congress Control Number: 2006911274

Table of Contents

All About Rain Forests

Tropical rain forests cover about 6 percent of the Earth. Temperatures there average about 75° **Fahrenheit** (24° C) each year.

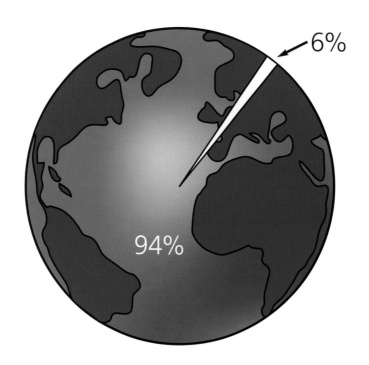

6%

94%

Tropical rain forests have an annual rainfall of about 80 inches (200 cm) a year. This climate makes them very wet and very warm places.

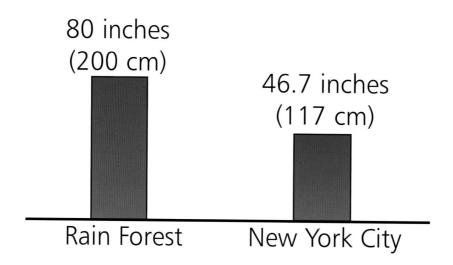

80 inches
(200 cm)

46.7 inches
(117 cm)

Rain Forest   New York City

Some **scientists** think thousands of **species** of plants and animals live in rain forests.

Where They Are

There are tropical rain forests in Southeast Asia and West Africa. There are smaller ones in Mexico, Central America, and northeastern Australia.

9

The most famous rain forest in
the world is in Brazil. It is also the
largest one.

This land is known as the Amazon rain forest, after the river that runs through it.

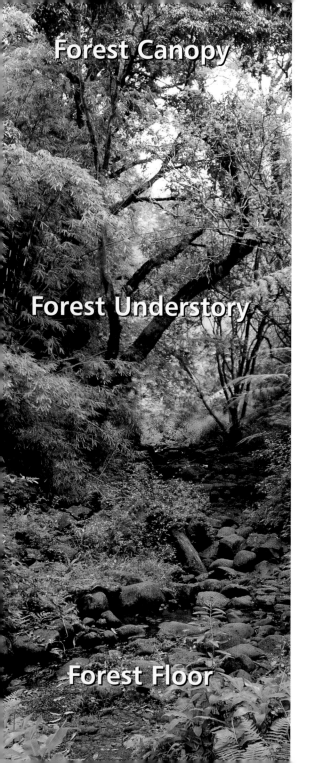

Forest Canopy

Forest Understory

Forest Floor

Inside a Rain Forest

The top of a rain forest is known as the **canopy**. The layer below the canopy is called the **understory**. Finally, there is the forest floor. Very little sunlight makes its way into the bottom layer.

Plant and Animal Life

Temperatures are warm all the time, so plants grow fast in rain forests. Mosses, vines, flowers, and trees grow well in a rain forest.

Most animals eat rain forest plants. Many birds, lizards, snakes, toads, and frogs are all found in rain forests.

The Future

Many native peoples live in rain forests. For a long time, they have made medicines from plants only found in rain forests.

19

Plants and trees have been cut down in many rain forests. The land that is left behind is no longer the same as it was. This harms many of the animals and plants that once lived there.

Many countries are trying to save the rain forests.
People do not want animals to become **extinct**.

Glossary

canopy (KAN uh pee) — the topmost layer of the rain forest

extinct (ek STINKT) — gone from the Earth forever

Fahrenheit (FAHR un hite) — one way of telling the temperature

scientists (SY un tists) — people who study plant and animal life

species (SPEE sheez) — certain kind of plant or animal within a closely related group

tropical (TROP uh kul) — pertaining to areas in the tropics

understory (UN der stor ee) — the middle layer of life in the rain forest

Index

FURTHER READING

Dell, Pamela. *Rain Forest Plants (Life in the World's Biomes)*. Bridgestone, 2005.
Kratter, Paul. *The Living Rain Forest: An Animal Alphabet*. Charlesbridge, 2004.
Parker, Edward. *Rain Forest People*. Raintree, 2002.

WEBSITES TO VISIT

Because Internet links change so often, Fitzgerald Books has developed an online list of websites related to the subject of this book. This site is updated regularly. Please use this link to access the list: www.fitzgeraldbookslinks.com/eh/rf

ABOUT THE AUTHOR

Ted O'Hare is an author and editor of children's nonfiction books. Ted has written over fifty children's books over the past decade. Ted has worked for many publishing houses including the Macmillan Children's Book Group.